The Big Hill

CARAMEL TREE

Chapter 1

BMX Bikes

Peter woke up to the sound of his alarm clock. It was Monday morning and time to get ready for school.

Peter was the most popular boy in grade five. Everybody liked him and wanted to be friends with him. When he walked across the school ground, he was never alone. Peter liked the attention and the feeling of being liked, but sometimes he did things just to make people like him.

When Peter got to school, he walked over to his friend Matt. Matt was a shy, small boy who was teased a lot by the other children in his class. He wanted to hang out with Peter because Peter was always nice to him. Matt never felt little when he was near Peter, even though Peter was much taller. The previous week, Peter had stood up for Matt in front of the whole class. Chuck, the class bully and two of his friends, had tried to catch Matt and put him into the garbage can, head first. Matt had felt ashamed, but Peter had been there for him and he stopped the bullies.

"So, how was your weekend, Peter?" Matt asked.
"I've been riding my bike a lot," Peter answered. He was wearing blue jeans, black runners, and a yellow T-shirt with a picture of a BMX bike on the back. He had a red and black baseball cap. His curly, brown hair just touched his shoulders; he didn't like it too long.

Sometimes he wore a shiny bracelet on his right wrist. His grandpa had given the bracelet to him on his eleventh birthday. He looked at it as a good luck charm.

"Sorry, Matt, but I have to go," Peter looked at his smaller classmate.

Matt looked up and said, "That's fine, see you in class."

Peter smiled at Matt, turned around and ran towards the gym. He stopped at a small group of boys from grade six and seven. Usually they wouldn't pay any attention to a 5th grader, but Peter was an exception and not only because he was tall.

Peter was a respected BMX bike rider. He was fearless when he was riding his bike in the pit. His fearlessness made him well known and highly respected in the BMX community. Just the other day, he challenged a grade six student at the bike pit. They had been on the edge of the pit, staring at each other, waiting for some of the younger riders to get out of their way. Then with a quick push, they jumped onto their bikes and shot down the steep wall. Peter had raced very well, and the older boys were very impressed.

"So what's up?" Peter asked. "Are you going to the bike pit after school tomorrow?"

"For sure," Chuck, the leader of the class bullies replied. He was bigger than Peter and a little bit fat. The jeans he wore were dirty, and there were food stains visible on his brown T-shirt. Two other boys were always with Chuck, and they were bullies, too. They were only brave when they were together.

"I want to race you again, Peter. This time, I'm going to beat you, and everyone will laugh at you," Chuck said with a mean look on his face.

"I will definitely come, but I have to do my homework first," answered Peter.

"That's your problem, but you sure would miss something," Chuck teased. "I would love to race you down the Big Hill, but I know you would never accept the challenge."

Peter was starting to get angry because he knew he could probably beat Chuck. Peter wanted to race Chuck soon, but he knew he would need to practice before he went down the Big Hill. He also knew that Chuck was just trying to make him mad and that arguing with three bullies was not a good idea. He decided to leave.

"Whatever," said Peter. "Like I said, see you tomorrow after school," added Peter as he got on his bike and started the trip home.

Chapter 2

The Pit

At school the next day, Peter sat at his desk staring at the clock. 2:59 p.m. Peter couldn't wait until school was over. As soon as the bell rang, he ran out of the building, jumped on his bike, and pedaled home as fast as he could.

'I will race Chuck today,' he thought with excitement as he dashed down the street and came

to a squeaking halt in front of his house. He had practiced braking hard and leaving a rubber mark on the road.

"Hi, Mom," he yelled when he ran into his house. "I'm going to the bike pit now. I'll be home at 6:00."

"Sorry, Peter," Mom said. "We have to go to your grandpa's house today. You know that it's his birthday."

Peter stopped half way up the stairs towards his bedroom. "Can't we go another time? I have to be at the bike pit in an hour."

"No. The bike pit won't go away, but your grandpa turns seventy five only once."

"But I..." Peter began but was interrupted.

"Don't argue. We are going. How about your homework?" Mom asked.

"Just some math and reading, so please can I go to the bike pit?" replied Peter.

"NO!" Mom said, "And NO means NO! Going to Grandpa's birthday is more important."

Peter was upset. He grumbled as he walked into his bedroom, slamming the door behind him with a loud bang.

He sat down at his desk and looked at the picture that Matt had taken two weeks ago. It showed Peter sitting on his BMX bike at the bike pit. The bike pit used to be an old gravel mine. The members of the club had changed it into an exciting bike-riding park with tall hills, sharp corners and high jumps. In the middle of the bike pit rose the Big Hill with its steep track.

The bike pit was Peter's favorite place. He spent hours practicing jumps, stops, and racing other kids.

Peter closed his eyes and dreamed about sitting on his bike on top of the Big Hill and getting ready to race down the steep path. He felt the wind rushing through his hair and the vibration of his bike as it crossed over the rough land.

He had never been on the Big Hill before. The club hadn't allowed him. The rules stated that children

below the age of twelve weren't allowed to ride the Big Hill. Even though Peter was one of the best riders, he couldn't convince the club's manager. It was too dangerous. During the championship rides the previous year, a fifteen-year-old boy had lost control over his bike and had crashed badly. He ended up in the hospital with broken bones.

'*One day, I will ride the Big Hill,*' Peter thought and opened his eyes, realizing that he was just sitting at his bedroom desk.

That evening, Peter and his family went to Grandpa's house. Peter was very fond of his grandpa. Occasionally, Peter would ride to his grandparents' house and spend the afternoon with them. They would talk about school and his daily routines, but Grandpa would also listen to Peter talk about the bike pit and what he was able to do on his bike. Grandpa had even come to the bike pit a few times to watch Peter ride. Peter had been very happy to see that Grandpa was interested in what he was doing besides school and homework.

Peter had a great time at his grandpa's birthday. After the party, Peter hugged his grandpa and said good night.

"Thank you, Peter," said Grandpa, "and be careful on your bike. Don't do anything dangerous."

Chapter 3

The Challenge

On Wednesday morning, Chuck and his two buddies were waiting for Peter in front of the school. Chuck waved his arms wildly when Peter entered the school ground.

"What happened to you yesterday?" He asked in a challenging way.

"I was at my grandpa's birthday party," Peter replied.

"Well, you missed all the excitement at the bike pit. Yesterday, there were no adults around at all, so the three of us went down the Big Hill together. It was awesome," Chuck bragged. "Where were you, I thought we were going to race?"

"Next time," Peter said calmly, even though he was filled with envy.

"You know Peter," Chuck continued, "I'm starting to think you're not as good as you pretend to be. Maybe you are just scared to go down the Big Hill. I think that I am the new BMX champion."

Now Peter was angry. He was very proud of what he could do on his BMX bike, and when he heard Chuck's words, his face turned red.

"Well, I'm going to prove you wrong," Peter said through clenched teeth. "Next time we race, I'm going to beat you, and we'll see who the real champion is!" Peter said as he stepped a little closer to the bullies. Chuck suddenly didn't seem as scary as yesterday.

"Are you sure you aren't too scared, you chicken?" Chuck laughed. "I'll tell everyone. It's a challenge. I can't wait to see this."

Chuck continued to laugh with his bully friends as they walked away from angry Peter.

The news that Peter had not come to the bike pit the day before spread fast and soon everyone knew. When Peter walked into his class, everybody looked at him.

Peter started to wonder if maybe some of the students were starting to think he was a chicken because he had not gone to the bike pit.

Chuck, who was standing at the door, said, "Hey chicken, we sure missed you yesterday. Ha, ha!" Peter ignored the comment and tried to forget about Chuck.

"You are not a chicken," Matt whispered. "Don't listen to Chuck. He doesn't know anything."

Peter smiled.

At lunch time, Peter sat with Matt on one of the picnic tables outside. It was warm and sunny, and most of the students were eating their lunches outside instead of in the cafeteria.

"Ah, gross!" said Matt as he looked at his sandwich.

"What?" replied Peter curiously.

"My mom put pickles in my sandwich again. I hate pickles," said Matt.

"Do you want to trade for my peanut butter sandwich?" Peter asked Matt. Peter loved pickles.

"Sure!" answered Matt sounding relieved. The boys exchanged sandwiches, and Peter took a big bite.

"Oh no. Not again," Matt said. Peter turned his head to see the three bullies walking over to their picnic table. "These guys just won't leave you alone."

"Hi, chicken. Are you ready for the race after school?" Chuck asked. He had ketchup on his face, and his shirt looked dirtier than usual.

"What race?" asked Peter slightly confused.

"The race after school, chicken," Chuck said.

"I didn't mean I wanted to race today. I thought that...I...I," Peter was surprised.

"Well, if you don't come today, EVERYONE will know you are a chicken. I told the whole class we are going to race down the Big Hill today after school. Everyone will be coming to cheer for me and see me beat you. See you there, chicken." Chuck and his bully friends laughed and made chicken noises as they walked away.

Peter looked at Matt without saying anything. Matt looked just as surprised as he was.

'What a sneaky trick,' Peter thought. He wanted to race down the Big Hill, but not today. It was too soon. He would need to practice first on some smaller hills for a few days before he decided to go down the Big Hill.

'What a mean bully,' he thought. 'Well, I guess now I don't have a choice.'

"I'm going to race him down the Big Hill today," said Peter after a few moments of silence. "I have to."

"No, you don't," replied Matt as the lunch bell rang. "He can't make you race him. You have to decide for yourself." Matt packed up his lunch box and walked inside.

Everyone started to walk back into the school. Peter sat by himself for a second. He opened the note his mom had left in the bottom of his lunch bag and read it as he walked into school.

'Have fun at the bike pit today and be safe.'

Chapter 4

The Big Hill

When the bell rang at the end of the school day, Peter walked out of the building to the bike rack to find Chuck sitting next to his bike.

"Hey, chicken. I just wanted to make sure you weren't going to run away again," he said. "Today is the big day. Are you ready to race me?"

"Oh, I'm ready," answered Peter. "I have to go home first to get my equipment," added Peter.

"Fine, then I'll see you there. Four o'clock, and don't be late, chicken-boy," Chuck yelled and clucked as he rode off.

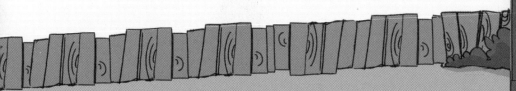

Peter's mind was racing as he rode home to prepare for the challenge with Chuck. When he got home, he walked into the garage to check out his blue BMX bike. The chain was tight, the front and rear brakes worked well, and the handlebars were set at the right distance. Peter looked closely at his bike seat to make sure it was in the right position. He noticed his tires were a little flat, so he got out his bike pump and added some air. He made sure he had his shin, knee, and elbow pads, and he put on his helmet. Once he was satisfied with his bike and protective gear, Peter checked to make sure he had his lucky bracelet on. He pushed the bike out of the garage and rode to the bike pit.

When he turned the last corner, he could already see the small crowd that had gathered at the entrance to the bike pit. He could see that almost everyone from school had come.

'This will be quite a show,' he thought.

When he got closer, he heard some people chanting his name. He pushed his bike through the crowd, and he heard encouraging words. His classmates patted him on the back.

"You can do it!" they yelled. "You are not a chicken! Show that bully what you can do!"

Once inside the bike pit, he spotted Chuck standing beside his orange BMX bike, smiling.

"So you came this time. Good for you. I thought you would chicken out again," Chuck said.

"Let's do it," Peter replied coldly.

Peter checked his protective gear again. He put on his elbow and knee pads, and he made sure his helmet was on securely. Finally, he put on his yellow gloves and grabbed the handlebars.

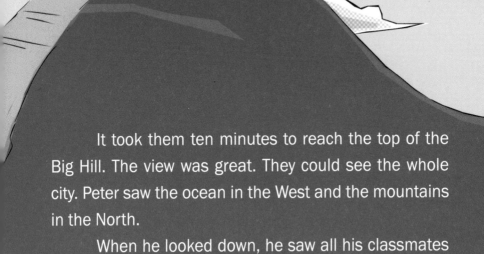

It took them ten minutes to reach the top of the Big Hill. The view was great. They could see the whole city. Peter saw the ocean in the West and the mountains in the North.

When he looked down, he saw all his classmates watching him, cheering and shouting. He could see Matt and some of his other friends. Then he looked beside him and saw Chuck; tall, big, mean and angry-looking.

Peter was a little nervous. He knew he probably should have practiced first on one of the smaller hills. The ride down looked much more difficult from the top of the Big Hill. Peter tried to focus. He concentrated intently. He studied the path he would take down the hill. He looked for rocks and hidden obstacles. The more he studied the hill, the more he wished he was somewhere else.

The wind picked up strength and swirled around Peter's face. It whistled in his ears and threw dust everywhere. Peter could feel his heart racing.

Suddenly, the voices of all his screaming classmates became one.

"TEN!...NINE!...EIGHT!...SEVEN!..." they yelled.

'Oh boy,' thought Peter. 'This is really happening.' Peter took a deep breath.

"SIX!... FIVE!...FOUR!...THREE!..."

Peter looked down the steep hill and saw the brown earth at the bottom of the bike pit. He closed his fingers around his handlebars, stepped with his right foot on the black pedal, and took a deep breath. Peter's mind began to clear. He gripped his handles tightly.

"TWO!...ONE!......GO!"

Peter jumped with his left foot on the other pedal and shot straight forward. Both riders flew through the air for a few seconds until their tires landed heavily on the dusty ground. The crowd cheered with a deafening sound.

Peter's legs were pedaling as fast as possible. He saw the ground come closer and closer, and the wind pushed into his face and tried to rip off his helmet. His stomach tightened, and blood rushed through his veins.

The two riders were side by side, focusing, racing faster than ever before. Peter was a wheel length ahead, and the crowd cheered wildly. Even Matt screamed with excitement.

Peter stepped hard onto the pedals, knowing that he could win, when something suddenly felt wrong. Peter looked down his front wheel and felt himself flipping through the air. His bike had hit a bump that

made him lose his balance. He saw the ground and then the sky, then he saw the crowd sideways and then the sky again, up was down and down was up.

Suddenly, everything stopped. Peter felt a sharp pain in his right arm, and his leg felt as if it was twisted around his body. Peter tried to keep his eyes open, but everything around him went dark.

Chapter 5

Consequences

When Peter opened his eyes, he had a bad headache, and everything around him was white. He was lying under white sheets, and his head rested on a white pillow.

"Peter, are you awake?" A familiar voice greeted him.

"Mom?" Peter asked carefully, every little movement hurt. "Where am I? What happened?"

"You are at the Central Hospital. You rode down the Big Hill and crashed," Mom said. "Why did you go down the Big Hill? You could have been killed!" Her eyes were red from crying, and her voice was filled with a sudden anger. She shook her head and got up from her chair. She walked closer and sat down gently on Peter's bed.

"I don't know," replied Peter slowly. "At the time, it seemed like I didn't have a choice."

"You always have a choice, Peter," Mom said.

"I am sorry, Mom," Peter said, realizing that his mother was right.

Peter was confused. He knew now that what he had done was foolish, but yesterday, he felt like he had to race.

"I guess I just didn't want to disappoint anyone," he said.

They talked for a while, and then his mother had to leave.

"I will be back tomorrow," she said and kissed him softly on his pale cheek. "You were lucky, my son, very lucky."

As Mom was leaving, Peter felt for his lucky bracelet but was shocked when it was not on his wrist.

'Oh no...' he thought, 'it must have fallen off when I crashed.' Peter was trying to think about how he could get his bracelet back but soon fell asleep.

Peter's night was restless and painful. He was in and out of sleep frequently, and he thought about his ride down the Big Hill.

He felt proud and sad at the same time. He had broken the rules by going on the Big Hill even though he was not twelve yet. Then he thought of his worst fear. *'What will all the kids think of me? They will probably all call me chicken forever,'* Peter thought, which only made him more restless. He tried to turn over, but it hurt too much so he decided to stay lying on his back.

In the middle of the night, a nurse came in to check on Peter. She gave him some medications and, after a while, he finally fell asleep.

Peter woke up on Thursday morning to hear a faint knock on the door. The door opened slowly, and Peter smiled as he saw Grandpa peeking through the opening.

"May I come in?" Grandpa asked.

"Hi, Grandpa," Peter replied happily. "Please come in."

Grandpa walked slowly into the room. "Hello, Peter," Grandpa said, as he sat down on the chair beside Peter's bed. "How are you doing?"

"A little bit better than yesterday, but still with lots of pain," Peter explained.

"I heard you rode down the Big Hill?" Grandpa opened his eyes wide but was still smiling.

"Yes," said Peter. "But I really think I shouldn't have. It's hard to say no when everyone is watching you."

"I know what you mean," Grandpa smiled.

"I hope you are not upset or disappointed," Peter said.

"I am not here to judge you, Peter. You have to deal with the consequences by yourself. All I can do is to be by your side," Grandpa assured.

Then Grandpa's face turned a little more serious. "Just tell me why you did it, Peter."

"I did it because..." Peter hesitated. "I am very good at BMX riding, you know, very good," he added.

"Well, that is probably true. So what did you want to prove by going down the Big Hill?" asked Grandpa.

"I guess I wanted to prove that I could win. If I hadn't hit that bump, I would have won," Peter said.

"So I hear," Grandpa smiled.

"But I didn't win," Peter sulked. "Worst of all, I know I raced just because I wanted to prove to everyone what a great BMX rider I am."

"I understand why you had to ride the Big Hill, and I hope you have learned a lesson. I think the pain that you feel is punishment enough," Grandpa said. Then he added, "You were lucky that you were wearing your helmet and the protective gear."

They talked for a while longer. Then there was a knock at the door. Grandpa walked to the door and called, "Come on in."

Peter stretched his neck as far as his pain would allow him and was happy to see Matt's smiling face.

"Hey, Peter," greeted Matt.

Peter tried to smile but immediately thought of his fear; the fear that had kept him up for most of the night. He asked Matt if everyone thought he was chicken.

"No way," replied Matt. "You did it! You raced down the Big Hill, and you would have won," Matt said excitedly.

"But I didn't win!" Peter sulked.

"Neither did Chuck," Matt said.

"What do you mean?" Peter was confused.

Matt walked closer to Peter's side and opened his hand. "Here," Matt said, handing over Peter's bracelet.

"My lucky bracelet!" Peter shouted. "Thanks, Matt."

"Don't thank me, thank Chuck," Matt explained. "He is the one who found your bracelet. He asked me to give it to you."

Peter looked confused. "So, Chuck didn't continue the race?" he asked.

"No," replied Matt. "Chuck stopped as soon as he saw you falling," Matt explained, "so no one won the race!"

"Chuck stopped when I fell?" Peter checked to see if he was hearing correctly.

"Yes. In fact, Chuck even wanted to ride in the ambulance with you," Matt said. "And he asked me to tell you that he will race you again after you get better. It turns out Chuck might not be such a bad guy after all."

Peter finally smiled. He was already thinking of when he could get back on his bike. He couldn't wait to get back to the bike pit and try the race again. He would soon turn twelve, and then he would be old enough to ride on the Big Hill without breaking the rules.

As he thought about it, he realized one important thing. Peter looked at Matt and Grandpa and said, "Next time, I'll race for myself and not because others expect me to."